WAIT UNTIL THEN

Tyndale House Publishers, Inc., Carol Stream, Illinois

Written by

RANDY ALCORN

Illustrated by DORON BEN-AMI

To our grandchildren,
Jacob Gary Stump,
Matthew James Franklin,
and Tyler Daniel Stump
—R. A.

*Trust in the LORD with all your heart;
do not depend on your own understanding.
Seek his will in all you do,
and he will show you which path to take.*

PROVERBS 3:5-6, NLT

To Grandpa Jerry,
who always hit a home run
into our hearts
—D. B.

Visit Tyndale's exciting Web site at www.tyndale.com

TYNDALE is a registered trademark of Tyndale House Publishers, Inc.

The Tyndale Kids logo is a trademark of Tyndale House Publishers, Inc.

Wait Until Then

Copyright © 2007 by Eternal Perspective Ministries. All rights reserved.

Cover and interior illustrations copyright © 2007 by Doron Ben-Ami. All rights reserved.

Edited by Betty Free Swanberg

Designed by Jacqueline L. Noe

Unless otherwise indicated, all Scripture quotations are taken from the *Holy Bible*, New International Version®. NIV®. Copyright © 1973, 1978, 1984 by International Bible Society. Used by permission of Zondervan. All rights reserved.

Scripture quotations marked NLT are taken from the *Holy Bible*, New Living Translation, copyright © 1996, 2004. Used by permission of Tyndale House Publishers, Inc., Carol Stream, Illinois 60188. All rights reserved.

Library of Congress Cataloging-in-Publication Data

Alcorn, Randy C.
  Wait until then / Randy Alcorn.
    p. cm.
  ISBN-13: 978-1-4143-1041-1 (hc)
  ISBN-10: 1-4143-1041-2 (hc)
  1. Children--Religious life. 2. Grandfathers--Religious life. 3. Grandparent and child--Religious aspects--Christianity. I. Title.
  BV4571.3.A43 2006
  248.8'2--dc22
                                2005033507

Printed in Singapore

13 12 11 10 09 08 07

7 6 5 4 3 2 1

Nathan loved baseball.

He went to baseball games. He watched baseball on TV. He enjoyed baseball movies, like *The Sandlot*. He read baseball books. He collected baseball cards. He talked about baseball with his family and friends.
He even dreamed about baseball.

But more than anything, Nathan loved to talk about baseball with his grandfather. Gramps had played second base for seven years in the minor leagues. And for one season he played in the majors, for the Boston Red Sox, with Ted Williams.

Gramps had lots of great stories.

"Joe DiMaggio is up, one out, man on first. I picture what's going to happen next. The ball would come to my right, I'd nab it, toss it, and the game would end on a double play."

"What happened, Gramps?"

Nathan knew the story as well as Gramps. But they both liked to pretend the story had never been told and never been heard.

"Joe smashes a grounder, the ball hits the arch of my left shoe, and it bounces to Billy Goodman at first. He throws the ball to second, and the game ends on a double play—right off my foot!"

Gramps laughed long and hard. Nathan laughed too.

"Gramps, can I see your baseball?" Nathan asked.

Gramps had more than one baseball. But he knew which one Nathan meant. He reached over to the glass case, opened it, and took the ball off the stand. He handed it to Nathan.

"That really is Ted Williams's signature, isn't it, Gramps?"

"Yep. It sure is. Baseball fans will never stop talking about Ted."

Nathan turned the ball over. "And here's your signature, Gramps, on the same ball with Ted Williams's."

Gramps said, "Of course, your grandpa wasn't nearly as good as Ted Williams, that's for sure." He chuckled.

"I bet you were, though," Nathan said.

"Well, thank you, Nathan. But you don't have to be the best player to love the game."

Nathan looked down. He felt sad.

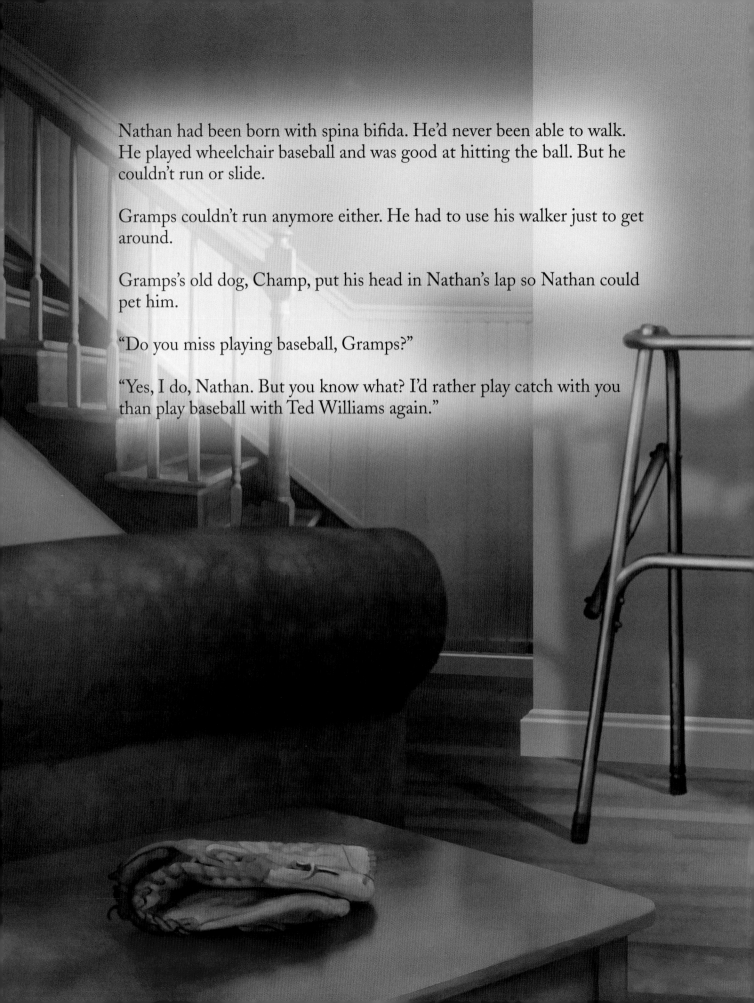

Nathan had been born with spina bifida. He'd never been able to walk. He played wheelchair baseball and was good at hitting the ball. But he couldn't run or slide.

Gramps couldn't run anymore either. He had to use his walker just to get around.

Gramps's old dog, Champ, put his head in Nathan's lap so Nathan could pet him.

"Do you miss playing baseball, Gramps?"

"Yes, I do, Nathan. But you know what? I'd rather play catch with you than play baseball with Ted Williams again."

When Gramps took Nathan to baseball games, they ate peanuts and popcorn.

One time two Dodgers came over to the third base line and signed baseball cards for Nathan. They were nice.

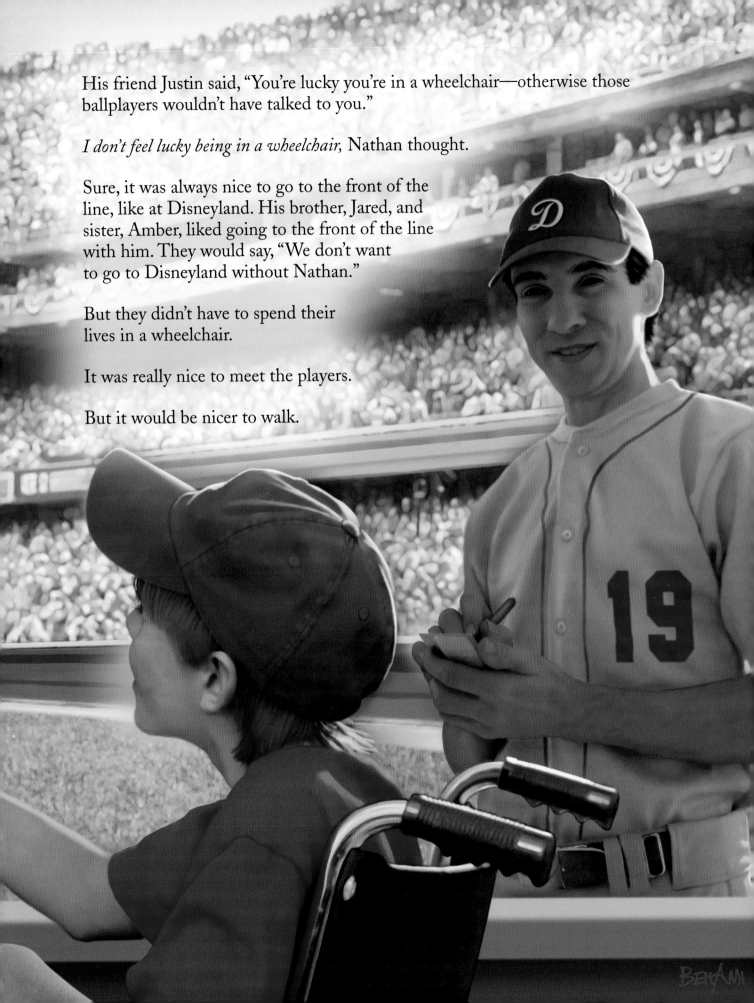

His friend Justin said, "You're lucky you're in a wheelchair—otherwise those ballplayers wouldn't have talked to you."

I don't feel lucky being in a wheelchair, Nathan thought.

Sure, it was always nice to go to the front of the line, like at Disneyland. His brother, Jared, and sister, Amber, liked going to the front of the line with him. They would say, "We don't want to go to Disneyland without Nathan."

But they didn't have to spend their lives in a wheelchair.

It was really nice to meet the players.

But it would be nicer to walk.

Gramps took Nathan fishing. Nathan liked to fish.

"This walker and I have become friends," Gramps said.
"We've been together three years."

Nathan wasn't sure if his wheelchair was a friend. He would
rather run and play real baseball like Gramps used to.

Gramps said, "I'm grateful for my baseball years. But they weren't
as important as other things—like marrying your grandma and
having children, including your mother.

"Baseball wasn't as important as working at the mill and being
a deacon at church and volunteering at the rescue mission.
And spending time with my grandson."

"But I still want to play baseball . . . and hit a
home run and actually run the bases."

"I know," Gramps said. "One day you will.
But you'll have to wait until then."

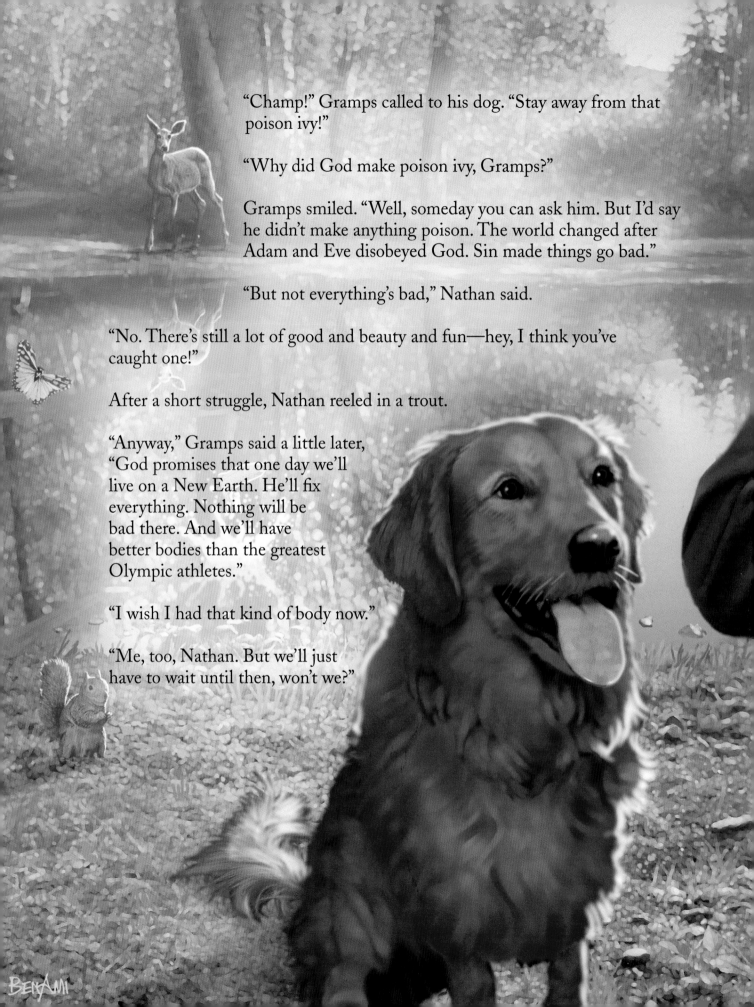

"Champ!" Gramps called to his dog. "Stay away from that poison ivy!"

"Why did God make poison ivy, Gramps?"

Gramps smiled. "Well, someday you can ask him. But I'd say he didn't make anything poison. The world changed after Adam and Eve disobeyed God. Sin made things go bad."

"But not everything's bad," Nathan said.

"No. There's still a lot of good and beauty and fun—hey, I think you've caught one!"

After a short struggle, Nathan reeled in a trout.

"Anyway," Gramps said a little later, "God promises that one day we'll live on a New Earth. He'll fix everything. Nothing will be bad there. And we'll have better bodies than the greatest Olympic athletes."

"I wish I had that kind of body now."

"Me, too, Nathan. But we'll just have to wait until then, won't we?"

"Will I play baseball without a wheelchair on the New Earth, Gramps? I mean, really?"

"Well, there's a lot I don't know. But I do know God is our Father, and fathers love to see their children play. Since we'll have new bodies on the New Earth, we know we'll be able to play baseball . . . and since they'll be better bodies, I'm pretty sure our best baseball is still ahead of us."

Gramps smiled.

Nathan nodded.

"You won't need your wheelchair, and I won't need my walker. I won't have cancer anymore either. I can hardly wait until then."

Nathan felt a lump in his throat. He didn't like the word *cancer*.

Three generations of Nathan's family sat around the table at Nathan's house. They prayed, ate dinner, laughed, and told stories. To Nathan, it felt like Thanksgiving.

"Gramps, who were some other great players on the Red Sox?" Jared asked.

"Let your grandfather eat," Mom said. But she was smiling because she knew Gramps.

"Dom DiMaggio, Joe's brother, was an all-star. And Vern Stephens had 159 RBIs the year I was with the Red Sox. That's as many as Ted Williams had."

"But not as many home runs," Nathan said.

"No. Not as many home runs." Gramps paused, then his eyes began to shine. "But there's someone else I know who's much greater than Ted Williams or Babe Ruth or any other baseball player there ever was. You know who I mean, don't you?"

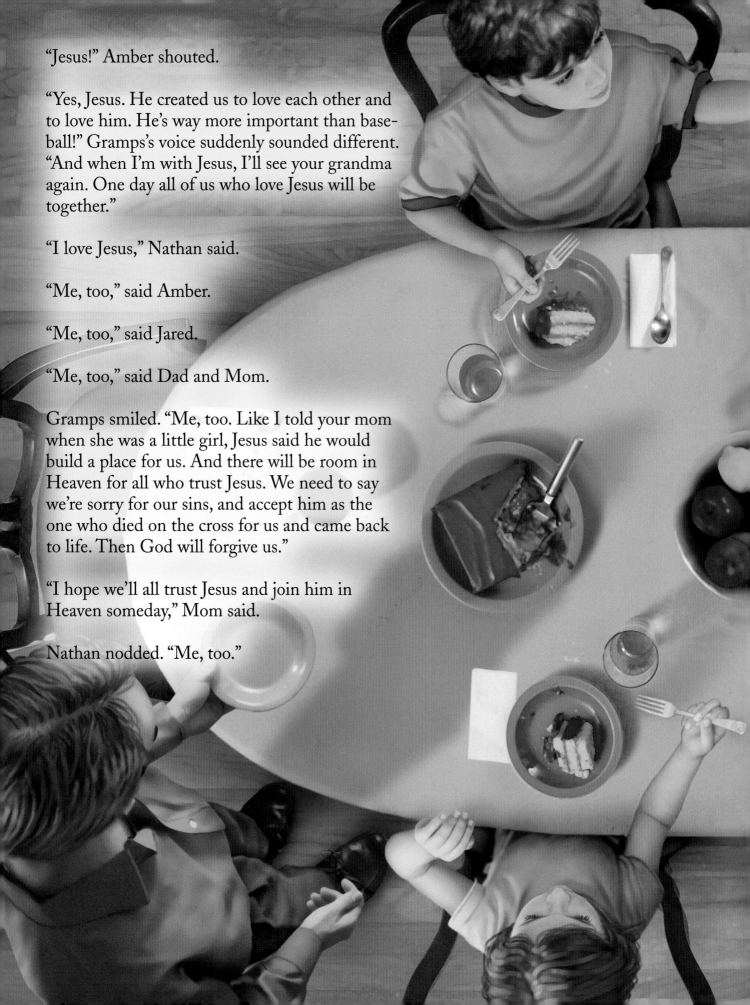

"Jesus!" Amber shouted.

"Yes, Jesus. He created us to love each other and to love him. He's way more important than baseball!" Gramps's voice suddenly sounded different. "And when I'm with Jesus, I'll see your grandma again. One day all of us who love Jesus will be together."

"I love Jesus," Nathan said.

"Me, too," said Amber.

"Me, too," said Jared.

"Me, too," said Dad and Mom.

Gramps smiled. "Me, too. Like I told your mom when she was a little girl, Jesus said he would build a place for us. And there will be room in Heaven for all who trust Jesus. We need to say we're sorry for our sins, and accept him as the one who died on the cross for us and came back to life. Then God will forgive us."

"I hope we'll all trust Jesus and join him in Heaven someday," Mom said.

Nathan nodded. "Me, too."

"Nathan," Gramps asked, "will you open to the last book of the Bible?"

Nathan wheeled his chair over to the coffee table and picked up the family Bible. He found Revelation and handed the Bible to Gramps.

Gramps read these words that Jesus said, from the end of the third chapter:

Here I am! I stand at the door and knock. If anyone hears my voice and opens the door, I will come in and eat with him, and he with me.

Closing the Bible, Gramps said, "Just like our family enjoys being together, Jesus wants us to enjoy being with him in God's family. Now and forever."

"Will he really live with us on the New Earth?" Nathan asked.

"Yes! And we'll eat delicious fruit from the tree of life. We'll have plenty to do. In fact, God will put us in charge of the whole earth, just the way he wanted it from the beginning! Jesus promises there will be no more sin or death or crying or pain. Do you believe him?"

"Yes!" Nathan said.

Nathan and Gramps went out to the deck to look at the stars. A meteor lit up the sky!

"Lots of kids with spina bifida can walk. Why didn't God make me so I could walk, Gramps?"

"I'm not sure, Nathan. But I know God has a good reason." Then Nathan and Gramps named a bunch of things Nathan could do.

"But on the New Earth we can play baseball whenever we want, right Gramps?"

"I wouldn't be surprised." Gramps laughed. "When I'm gone, Nathan, it'll be your job to remind everybody about Jesus and the New Earth! If anyone seems unhappy, just tell them to wait until then."

Nathan swallowed hard. He didn't like Gramps saying, "When I'm gone."

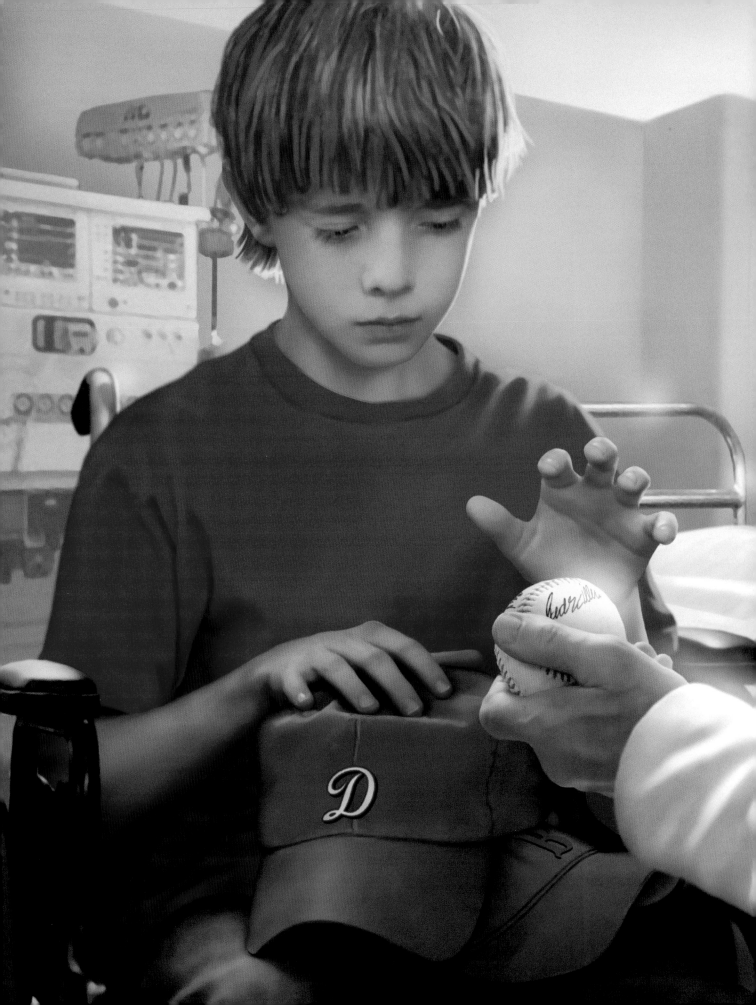

Two weeks later when Nathan came home from school, he knew something was wrong.

"We had to take Gramps to the hospital," Mom said. "His cancer is . . . worse. Do you want to go see him?"

When they arrived, Gramps was in a hospital bed. He smiled, but he seemed very weak.

"Nathan, I want you to love Jesus and pray to him every day. It's fine to enjoy baseball. But remember, everything we love should cause us to love Jesus more, not less."

Nathan nodded.

"Don't forget, one day God will make us what we should be and the whole earth what it should be. We just have to wait until then."

Nathan nodded again.

"I'm giving you this baseball," Gramps said, handing it to him. "I know you'll take good care of it." Nathan stared at the old baseball, then looked into his grandfather's eyes.

"I love you, Nathan."

"I love you, Gramps."

Soon Gramps couldn't talk. A week later, he died.

At the memorial service, the pastor said that Gramps loved Jesus and prayed for others and helped poor people.

Nathan's dad read something from each of the grandchildren. Nathan's note said, "Gramps told me about baseball. He always played catch with me. And he told me about Jesus and Heaven."

People told funny stories about Gramps that made everyone laugh and cry.

As they drove home, Nathan asked his father, "Do you think Gramps is playing baseball yet?"

"Well, we know he's having a good time with Jesus. But I don't think he'll play baseball until Jesus comes back to earth. Then our bodies will be raised up strong and healthy, and all of us can play with Gramps."

Nathan turned the baseball over in his hand. He went right past the signature of Ted Williams and found his grandfather's. Nathan held the baseball close. He traced Gramps's name with his finger and said, "I guess . . . we'll just have to wait until then."

I saw a new heaven and a new earth....
And I heard a loud voice from the throne
saying, "Now the dwelling of God is
with men, and he will live with them....
He will wipe every tear from their eyes.
There will be no more death or mourning
or crying or pain.
Revelation 21:1, 3–4

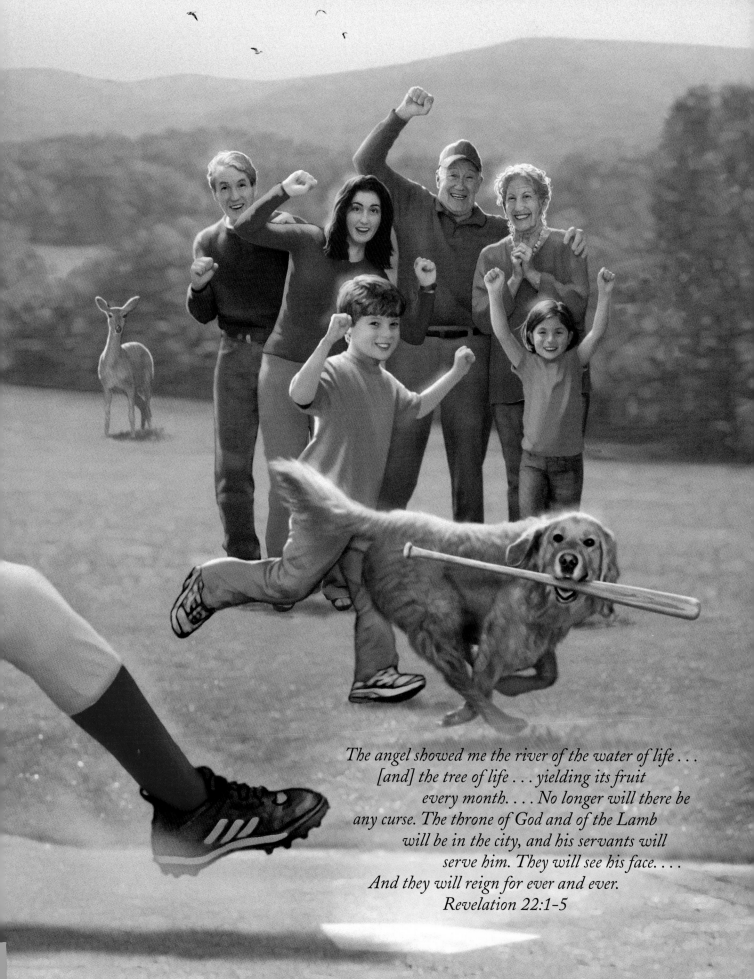

The angel showed me the river of the water of life . . .
[and] the tree of life . . . yielding its fruit
every month. . . . No longer will there be
any curse. The throne of God and of the Lamb
will be in the city, and his servants will
serve him. They will see his face. . . .
And they will reign for ever and ever.
Revelation 22:1-5

NOTE TO PARENTS, GRANDPARENTS, AND OTHER ADULTS

My prayer is that this book provides you an opportunity to talk about Jesus and Heaven to the children you love. I pray also that it helps you lead children to faith in Jesus, the King of kings. Ask the Holy Spirit to make you sensitive to the needs and interests of the children in your life. Then share some of the following points whenever it seems appropriate—especially after reading the book together.

The World God Made

- God made the earth, the sun and moon, and all the stars and planets. And he made the animals, then Adam and Eve. He put them in the beautiful Garden of Eden to work and rule the earth and to enjoy God and each other. It was a perfect place. (See Genesis 1–2.)

- Adam and Eve sinned by disobeying God. This is known as the Fall. Now we are under the Curse. People—and the earth—are no longer perfect. (See Genesis 3.) This is all because of our sin. God is perfectly holy, so he couldn't let people get away with sinning. Adam and Eve had to leave the Garden, and work became harder. Suddenly there was suffering and death. Minds and hearts and bodies didn't work right anymore. It was very sad.

- God never gave up his original plan. That plan is for people who love and obey him to rule a perfect earth, like the one God originally created.

Jesus and Us

- Jesus, God's Son, came from Heaven to earth. He became a human being and grew up to be a carpenter. Carpenters make things and fix things. Someday Jesus will fix us up so we'll be perfect forever. He will make the earth perfect forever too! Jesus said that everything will be made like new again (see Matthew 19:28 and Revelation 21:5).

- Jesus loves us so much that he died on the cross for our sins. Then he came back to life. That's called his resurrection. When we believe that this is true and ask Jesus to forgive us, he becomes our Savior!

- We can let Jesus take charge of our lives because he knows what's best for us. (Sometimes that includes difficult things, such as having a disability or sad things happening.) Letting Jesus be our King means we can enjoy having him as our friend and leader, now and forever.

Heaven and Us

- When people die, those who know Jesus as their Savior and King will go to Heaven. Life there is much better than it is here and now (see Philippians 1:21-23).

- When people we love go to Heaven, we feel sad because we miss them. But we can be happy that they are in a wonderful place. If we love Jesus, we will see them again and live with them forever. (I don't think that those who die old will look old, as in the book's final scene. We did this only to make it clear who the characters are.)

- After Jesus comes back to earth, Heaven will be even more wonderful, because God will come down to live with us in a perfect New Earth. Even animals will no longer suffer. (See Romans 8:19-21.) It will be like the Garden of Eden, but better. Nothing bad or sad will be there (see Revelation 20:10; 21:1-4).

- On the New Earth we will eat and laugh and play. We will have resurrection bodies like Jesus has (see Philippians 3:20-21). We know Jesus has a physical body, because after his resurrection he ate and let people touch him. He said, "A ghost does not have flesh and bones, as you see I have" (see Luke 24:38-43).

- There will be a great city, the New Jerusalem, where we will worship God and serve him and rule the earth with him forever (see Revelation 21:1-2; 22:3-5). This means that we will never be bored. There will always be fun and exciting things to do! We will do what people were made to do—worship and talk and walk and eat and run and play and rest.

- People of all different races and nations will be on the New Earth, and they will bring beautiful things to God, the King on the throne in the New Jerusalem (see Revelation 21:23-26). Since God will live there, the New Earth will be at the center of Heaven.

- The tree of life, which was in the Garden of Eden, will be there, and we will eat from it (see Revelation 2:7; 22:1-2).

- God will live with us, and we'll never cry or get sick or have pain or disabilities (see Revelation 21:3-4). We'll live forever with Jesus, the *person* we were made for, and we'll live in Heaven, the *place* we were made for!